CONTENTS

Little Red Riding Hood

By the Brothers Grimm

ONCE UPON A TIME there was a dear little girl who was loved by everyone who looked at her, but most of all by her grandmother, and there was nothing that she would not have given to the child. Once she gave her a little riding hood of red velvet, which suited the little girl so well that she would never wear anything else; so from that day forward she was always called "Little Red Riding Hood".

One day her mother said to her: "Come, Little Red Riding Hood, here is a piece of cake and a bottle of wine; take them to your grandmother. She is ill and weak, and they will do her good. Set out before it gets hot, and when you are going, walk nicely and quietly and do not run off the path, or you may fall and break the bottle; and when you go into her room, don't forget to say, 'Good morning,' and don't peep into every corner before you do it."

"I will take great care," said Little Red Riding Hood to her mother, and gave her hand on it.

The grandmother lived out in the wood, half a league from the village, and just as Little Red Riding Hood entered the wood, a wolf met her. She did not know what a wicked creature he was, and was not at all afraid of him.

"Good day, Little Red Riding Hood," said he.

"Thank you kindly, wolf."

"Whither away so early, Little Red Riding Hood?"

"To my grandmother's."

"What have you got in your apron?"

"Cake and wine; yesterday was baking-day, so poor sick grandmother is to have something good, to make her stronger."

"Where does your grandmother live, Little Red Riding Hood?"

"A good quarter of a league farther on in the wood; her house stands under the three large oak-trees, the nut-trees are just below; you surely must know it," replied Little Red Riding Hood.

The wolf thought to himself: 'What a tender

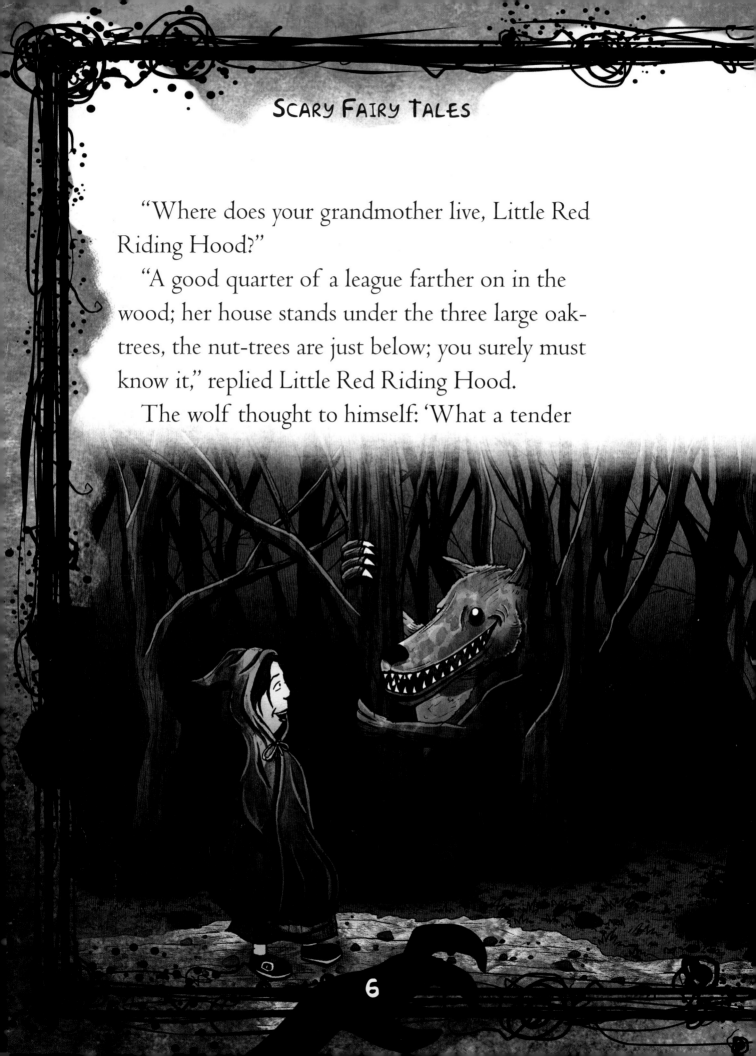

young creature! What a nice plump mouthful! She will be better to eat than the old woman. I must act craftily, so as to catch both.'

So he walked for a short time by the side of Little Red Riding Hood, and then he said: "See, Little Red Riding Hood, how pretty the flowers are about here – why do you not look round? I believe, too, that you do not hear how sweetly the little birds are singing; you walk gravely along as if you were going to school, while everything else out here in the wood is merry."

Little Red Riding Hood raised her eyes, and when she saw the sunbeams dancing here and there through the trees, and pretty flowers growing everywhere, she thought: 'Suppose I take grandmother a fresh nosegay; that would please her too. It is so early in the day that I shall still get there in good time.'

So she ran from the path into the wood to look for flowers. And whenever she had picked one, she fancied that she saw a still prettier one farther on, and ran after it, and so Little Red Riding Hood got deeper and deeper into the wood.

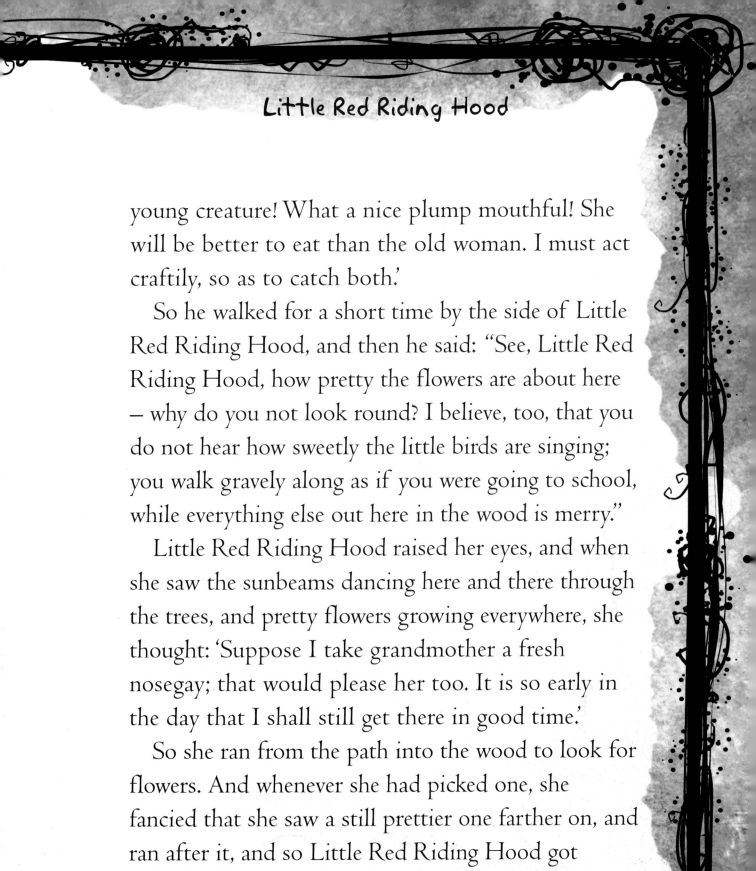

Meanwhile the wolf ran straight to the grandmother's house and knocked at the door.

"Who is there?"

"Little Red Riding Hood," replied the wolf. "She is bringing cake and wine; open the door."

"Lift the latch," called out the grandmother, "I am too weak, and cannot get up."

The wolf lifted the latch, the door sprang open, and without saying a word he went straight to the grandmother's bed and devoured her. Then he put on her clothes, dressed himself in her cap, laid himself in the bed and drew the curtains.

Little Red Riding Hood, however, had been running about picking flowers, and when she had gathered so many that she could carry no more, she remembered her grandmother, and set out on the way to her.

She was surprised to find the cottage door standing open, and when she went into the room, she had such a strange feeling that she said to herself: "Oh dear! How uneasy I feel today, and at other times I like

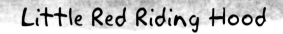

being with grandmother so much." She called out: "Good morning," but received no answer; so she went to the bed and drew back the curtains. There lay her grandmother with her cap pulled far over her face, and looking very strange.

"Oh, Grandmother," Little Red Riding Hood said, "what big ears you have!"

"All the better to hear you with," was the reply.

"But, Grandmother, what big eyes you have!"

"All the better to see you with."

"But, Grandmother, what large hands you have!"

"All the better to hug you with."

"Oh but, Grandmother, what a terrible big mouth you have!"

"All the better to eat you with!"

And scarcely had the wolf said this, than with one bound he was out of the bed and had swallowed up Little Red Riding Hood.

When the wolf had appeased his appetite, he lay down again in the bed, fell asleep and began to snore very loudly.

A huntsman was just passing the house, and thought to himself: 'How the old woman is snoring! I must just see if she wants anything.' So he went into the room, and when he came to the bed, he saw that the wolf was lying in it.

"Do I find you here, you monster!" said he. "I have long sought you!" But just as he was going to fire at him, it occurred to him that the wolf might have devoured the grandmother, and that she might still be saved. So he did not fire, but took a pair of scissors, and began to cut open the stomach of the sleeping wolf.

When the huntsman had made two snips, he saw the little red riding hood shining, and then he made two more snips, and the little girl sprang out, crying: "Ah, how frightened I have been! How dark it was inside the wolf."

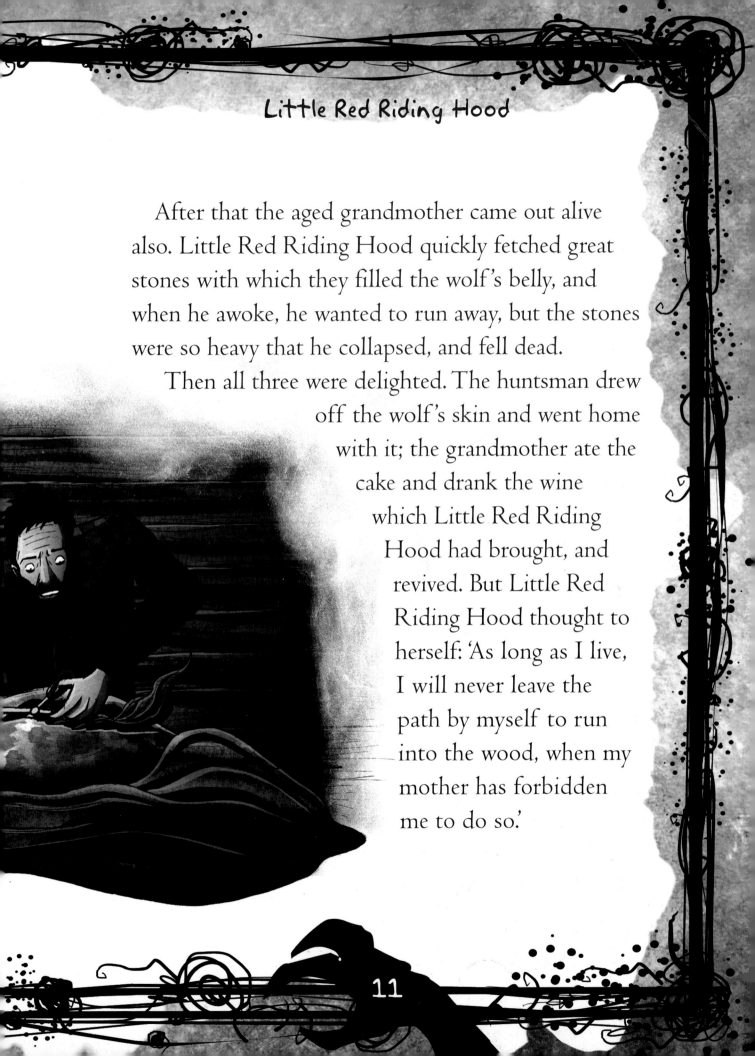

After that the aged grandmother came out alive also. Little Red Riding Hood quickly fetched great stones with which they filled the wolf's belly, and when he awoke, he wanted to run away, but the stones were so heavy that he collapsed, and fell dead.

Then all three were delighted. The huntsman drew off the wolf's skin and went home with it; the grandmother ate the cake and drank the wine which Little Red Riding Hood had brought, and revived. But Little Red Riding Hood thought to herself: 'As long as I live, I will never leave the path by myself to run into the wood, when my mother has forbidden me to do so.'

Schippeitaro

From *Tales of Wonder Every Child Should Know*,
by Kate Douglas Wiggin and Nora Archibald Smith

Long, long ago, in the days of fairies and giants,
ogres and dragons, valiant knights and distressed
damsels; in those days, a brave young warrior went
out into the wide world in search of adventures.

He travelled over hill and down dale, and for some
time he went on without meeting anything out of the
ordinary, but at length, after journeying through a
thick forest, he found himself, one evening, on a wild
and lonely mountain side. No village was in sight, no
cottage, not even the hut of a charcoal burner, so
often to be found on the outskirts of the forest. He

had been following a faint path, but at length, even that was lost sight of in the dense undergrowth.

Twilight was coming on, and in vain he strove to recover the lost track. Each effort seemed only to entangle him more hopelessly in the briers, thick ferns and tall grasses which grew on all sides. Faint and weary he stumbled on in the fast gathering darkness, until suddenly he came upon an eerie little temple, deserted and half ruined, but which still contained a shrine. Here at least was shelter from the chill and, though the sinister appearance made the hairs on the back of his neck stand up, here he resolved to pass the night. Wrapped in his thick mantle, and with his good sword by his side, he lay down, and was soon fast asleep.

Toward midnight he was awakened by a dreadful noise. At first he thought it must be a dream, but the rumpus continued, the whole place resounding with the most terrible shrieks and yells. The young warrior raised himself cautiously, and seizing his sword, peeped quietly through a hole in the ruined wall. He

beheld a strange and awful sight. A troop of hideous cats were engaged in a wild and horrible dance, their howling meanwhile echoing through the night. Mingled with their unearthly cries the young warrior could clearly distinguish the words:

"Tell it not to Schippeitaro! Listen for his bark!
Tell it not to Schippeitaro! Keep it close and dark!"

A clear full moon shed its light upon this gruesome scene, which the bold young warrior watched with amazement and horror. Suddenly, the midnight hour being passed, the phantom cats

disappeared, and all was silent once more.

The rest of the night passed undisturbed, and the young warrior slept soundly until morning. When he awoke the sun was already up, and he hastened to leave the strange scene of last night's adventure. He presently discovered traces of a path which the evening before had been invisible. This he followed, and found to his great joy, that it led, not as he had feared, to the forest through which he had come, but in the opposite direction, toward an open plain. There he saw one or two scattered cottages, and, a little farther on, a village.

Pressed by an awful hunger that was gnawing away at his stomach, he was making his way toward the village, when he heard the tones of a woman's voice loud in wailing and pleading. No sooner did these sounds of distress reach the warrior's ears, than his hunger was forgotten, and he hurried on to the nearest cottage, to find out what was the matter and if he could give any help. The people, shaking their heads sorrowfully, told him that all help was in vain.

"Every year," said they, "the mountain spirit claims a victim. The time has come, and this very night he will devour our loveliest maiden. This is the cause of all our weeping and gnashing of teeth." And when the young warrior enquired further, they told him that at sunset the victim would be put into a cage, carried to that very ruined temple where he had passed the night, and there left alone. In the morning she would have vanished. So it was each year, and so it would be now; there was no help for it.

The young warrior had a noble heart, and as he listened he was filled with an earnest desire to deliver the maiden. And, the mention of the ruined temple having brought back to his mind the adventure of the night before, he asked the people whether they had ever heard the name of Schippeitaro, and who and what he was. "Schippeitaro is a strong and beautiful dog," was the reply; "he belongs to the head man of our prince who lives only a little way from here. We often see him following his master; he is a fine and brave fellow."

The young knight did not stop to ask more questions, but hurried off to Schippeitaro's master and begged him to lend his dog for one night. The dog's master listened carefully to the warrior's strange tale. At length, he agreed to lend Schippeitaro on condition that he should be brought back the next day. Overjoyed, the young warrior led the dog away.

Next he went to see the parents of the unhappy maiden who was to be left out for the sacrifice. The warrior told them to keep their daughter safely in the house and watch her carefully until his return. He then placed the dog Schippeitaro in the cage which had been prepared for the maiden; and, with the help of some of the young men of the village, carried it to the ruined temple. The young men refused to stay one moment, but hurried down the mountain as if the whole troop of hobgoblins had been at their heels. The young warrior, with no companion but the dog, remained to see what would happen.

The valiant knight waited alone in the dark and the cold, alert for any snap of twig or rustle of undergrowth. He waited, watched and listened, listened, watched and waited, until at midnight, when the full moon was high in the heaven, the phantom cats came once more. This time they had in their midst a huge, black tom-cat, fiercer and more terrible than all the rest, which the young warrior had no difficulty in knowing as the mountain fiend himself. No sooner did this monster catch sight of the cage than he danced and sprang round it with yells of triumph and hideous joy, followed by his companions. When he had long enough taunted his victim, he threw open the door of the cage.

But this time he met his match. The brave Schippeitaro sprang upon him, and held him fast with his teeth, while the young warrior with one stroke of his good sword laid the monster dead at his feet. As for the other cats, they stood gazing at the dead body of their leader, and were made short work of by the knight and Schippeitaro. The young warrior brought back the brave dog to his master, with a thousand thanks, told the father and mother of the

maiden that their daughter was free, and told the
people of the village that the fiend would trouble
them no more. "You owe all this to the brave
Schippeitaro," he said as he bade them farewell, and
went his way in search of fresh adventures.

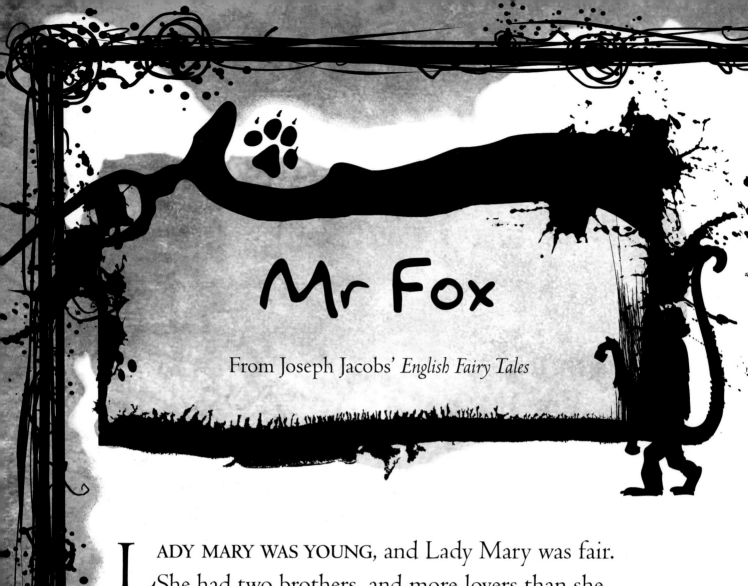

Mr Fox

From Joseph Jacobs' *English Fairy Tales*

LADY MARY WAS YOUNG, and Lady Mary was fair. She had two brothers, and more lovers than she could count. But of them all, the bravest and most gallant, was a Mr Fox, whom she met when she was down at her father's country house. No one knew who Mr Fox was; but he was certainly brave, and surely rich, and of all her lovers, Lady Mary cared for him alone. At last it was agreed upon between them that they should be married. Lady Mary asked Mr Fox where they should live, and he described to her his castle, and where it was; but, strange to say, did not ask her, nor her brothers, nor her friends, to come and see it.

So one day, near the wedding day, when her brothers were out, and Mr Fox was away for a day or two on business, as he said, Lady Mary set out for Mr Fox's castle. She journeyed up into the foothills of towering mountains, and after many searchings among crevices and crags, she came at last to it, and a fine, strong house it was, with towering, thick walls and a deep moat. And when she came up to the gateway she saw written on it:

Be Bold, Be Bold.

But as the gate was open, she went through it, and found no one there. So she went up to the doorway, and over it she found written:

Be Bold, Be Bold, But Not Too Bold.

Still she went on, till she came into the hall, and went up the broad stairs till she came to a door in the gallery, over which was written:

Be Bold, Be Bold, But Not Too Bold, Lest
That Your Heart's Blood Should Run Cold.

But Lady Mary was a brave one, and she opened
the door. She saw bodies and skeletons of young
ladies all stained with blood! So Lady Mary thought
it was time to get out of that place, and she closed
the door, went through the gallery, and was just going
down the stairs and out of the hall, when she saw
Mr Fox through the window, dragging a young lady
along from the gateway to the door. Lady Mary
rushed downstairs, and hid herself behind a cask, just
in time, as Mr Fox came in with the poor young lady
who seemed to have fainted. Just as he got near
Lady Mary, Mr Fox saw a diamond ring glittering on
the finger of the young lady he was dragging, and he
tried to pull it off. But it was tightly fixed, and would
not come off, so Mr Fox drew his sword, raised it,
and brought it down upon the hand of the poor lady.
The sword cut off the hand, which jumped up into
the air, and fell of all places in the world into Lady
Mary's lap. Imagine her horror! But somehow she
managed not to jump or shriek — she didn't move so
much as an inch or let out so much as a gasp. Mr Fox

looked about a bit for the dripping, oozing hand, but did not think of looking behind the cask, so at last he went on dragging the young lady up the stairs into the Bloody Chamber.

As soon as she heard him pass through the gallery, Lady Mary crept out of the door, down through the gateway, and ran home as fast as she could.

Now it happened that the very next day the marriage contract of Lady Mary and Mr Fox was to be signed, and there was a splendid breakfast before that with their families and all their friends. When Mr Fox was seated at the table opposite Lady Mary, he looked at her. "How pale you are this morning, my dear," he soothed.

"Yes," said she, "I had a bad night's rest last night. I had horrible dreams."

"Dreams always mean the opposite of what they seem," said Mr Fox; "but tell us your dream, and I shall do my best to interpret. Whether I can or not, your sweet voice will make the time pass till the happy hour comes."

"I dreamed," said Lady Mary, "that I went to your castle yesterday morning, and I found it in the woods, with high walls, and a deep moat, and on the gateway was written: *Be Bold, Be Bold.*"

"But it is not so, nor it was not so," said Mr Fox.

"And when I came to the doorway over it was written: *Be Bold, Be Bold, But Not Too Bold.*"

"It is not so, nor it was not so," said Mr Fox.

"And then I went upstairs, and came to a gallery, at the end of which was a door, over which was written: *Be Bold, Be Bold, But Not Too Bold, Lest That Your Heart's Blood Should Run Cold.*"

"It is not so, nor it was not so," said Mr Fox.

"And then — and then I opened the door, and the room was filled with bodies and skeletons of poor dead women, all stained with their blood."

"It is not so, nor it was not so. And God forbid it should be so," said Mr Fox.

"I then dreamed that I rushed down the gallery, and just as I was going down the stairs, I saw you, Mr Fox, coming up to the hall door, dragging after you a poor young lady, rich and beautiful."

"It is not so, nor it was not so. And God forbid it should be so," said Mr Fox.

"I rushed downstairs, just in time to hide myself behind a cask, when you, Mr Fox, came in dragging the young lady by the arm. And, as you passed me, I thought I saw you try and get off her diamond ring, and when you could not, Mr Fox, it seemed to me in my dream, that you got out your sword and hacked off the poor lady's hand to get the ring."

"It is not so, nor it was not so. And God forbid it should be so," said Mr Fox. He was going to say something else as he rose from his seat, when Lady Mary cried out: "But it is so, and it was so. Here's the hand and ring I have to show." She pulled out the lady's hand from her dress, and pointed it straight at Mr Fox.

At once her brothers and her friends drew their swords and cut Mr Fox into a thousand pieces.

The Farmer and the Badger

From *Japanese Fairy Tales* by Yei Theodora Ozaki

Long, long ago in the distant country of Japan, there lived an old farmer and his wife who had made their home in the mountains, far from any town. Their only neighbour was a bad and malicious badger. This badger used to come out every night, whether moonlit or dark, and run across to the farmer's field and spoil the vegetables and the rice which the farmer spent his time carefully cultivating. The badger at last grew so ruthless in his mischievous work, and did so much harm everywhere on the farm, that the good-natured farmer could not stand it any longer, and determined to put a stop to it. So he laid traps for the wicked animal.

The farmer's trouble and patience was rewarded, for one fine day on going about his rounds he found the badger caught in a hole he had dug and disguised. The farmer was delighted at having caught his enemy, and carried him home securely bound with rope. When he reached the house the farmer said to his wife: "I have at last caught the bad badger. You must keep an eye on him while I am out at work and not let him escape, because I want to get my revenge and have hot badger soup for supper tonight." Saying this, he hung the badger up to the rafters of his storehouse and went out to his work in the fields.

The badger was in great distress, for he did not at all like the idea of being made into soup, and he thought and thought for a long time, trying to hit upon some plan by which he might escape. It was hard to think clearly in his position, for he had been hung upside down. Very near him, at the entrance to the storehouse, looking out towards the green fields,

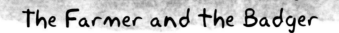

stood the farmer's old wife, pounding barley with a huge wooden pestle. Her face was seamed with many wrinkles, and was as brown as leather, and every now and then, she stopped to wipe the perspiration which rolled down her face. As the badger watched her, a wicked plan formed in his evil mind.

"Dear lady," said the wily badger, "you must be very weary doing such heavy work in your old age. Won't you let me do that for you? My arms are very strong, and I could relieve you for a little while so you can rest."

"Thank you for your kindness," said the old woman, "but I cannot let you do this work for me because I must not untie you, for you might escape if I did, and my husband would be very angry."

Now, the badger is one of the most cunning of animals, and he said in a very sad, gentle voice: "You are very unkind. You might untie me, for I promise not to try to escape. If you are afraid of your husband, I will let you bind me again before his return. I am so tired and sore tied up like this. If you would only let me down for just a few minutes I would indeed be very thankful!"

The old woman had a good and simple nature, and could not think badly of anyone. Much less did she think that the badger was only deceiving her. She felt sorry, too, for the animal as she turned to look at him. So in the kindness of her heart, and believing the creature's promise that he would not run away, she untied the rope and let the badger down.

The old woman then gave him the big, heavy pestle and told him to do the work for a short time while she rested. He took the solid piece of wood, but instead of doing the work, the badger at once sprang upon the old woman and knocked her down with it. He then killed her and cut her up and made soup of her in her own kitchen. But even then the bad badger didn't escape to freedom. Oh no, he was more wicked than that. Instead he stayed and waited for the return of the old farmer.

The old man worked hard in his fields all day, and as he worked he thought with pleasure that no more now would his labour be spoiled by the destructive badger. Towards sunset he left his work and turned to go home. He was very tired, but the thought of the nice supper of hot badger soup cheered him. The thought that the badger might get free and take revenge never once came into his mind.

He also never imagined that the badger knew magic. But of course, he did. And while the man was tramping home, the badger used his dark arts to take on the old woman's shape. As soon as he saw the farmer approaching he came out to greet him on the veranda, saying: "So you have come back at last. I have made the badger soup and have been waiting for you for a long time."

The old farmer quickly took off his straw sandals and sat down before his dinner-tray. The innocent man never even dreamed that it was not his wife but the badger who was waiting upon him, and asked at once for the soup.

Then the badger suddenly transformed himself back to his natural form and cried out: "You wife-

eating old man! Look out for the bones in the kitchen!" Laughing scornfully he escaped out of the house and ran away to his den in the hills.

The old man was left behind alone. He was stunned into silence. As he realised what must have happened, and the whole truth sunk in, he was so scared and horrified that he fainted right away. After a while he came round and burst into tears. He rocked himself to and fro in his hopeless grief. It seemed too terrible to be real that his faithful old wife had been killed and cooked by the badger while he was working quietly in the fields, knowing nothing of what was going on, and congratulating himself on having once and for all got rid of the wicked animal. And oh! The horrible thought; he had very nearly drunk the soup which the creature had made of his poor old woman. "Oh dear, oh dear, oh dear!" he wailed aloud, clutching at himself and shaking his head in horror.

Now, not far away there lived in the same mountain a kind, good-natured old rabbit. He heard the old man crying and sobbing and at once set out to see what was the matter, and if there was anything he could do to help. The old man told him all that had happened. When the rabbit heard the story he was very angry at the wicked and deceitful badger, and told the old man to leave everything to him and he would avenge his wife's death. The farmer was at last comforted, and, wiping away his tears, thanked the rabbit for his goodness in coming to him in his distress. The rabbit, seeing that the farmer was growing calmer, went back to his home to lay his plans for the punishment of the badger – for he was also very wise, as well as kind.

The next day the rabbit went out to find the badger. The evil creature was not to be seen in the woods or on the hillside or in the fields anywhere, so the rabbit went to his den and found the badger hiding there. Despite his dark magic powers, the animal had been afraid to show himself ever since he had escaped from the farmer's house, for fear of the old man's wrath.

The rabbit called out: "Why are you not out on such a beautiful day? Come out with me, and we will go and cut grass on the hills together."

The badger, never doubting but that the gentle rabbit was his friend, willingly consented to go out with him, only too glad to get away from the neighbourhood of the farmer and the fear of meeting him or being trapped once again. The rabbit led the way miles from their homes, out on the hills where the grass grew tall and thick and sweet. They both set to work to cut down as much as they could carry home, to store it up for their winter's food. When they had each cut down all they wanted they tied it in bundles and then started homewards, each carrying his bundle of grass on his back. This time the rabbit made the badger go first.

When they had gone a little way the rabbit took out a flint and steel, and, striking it over the badger's back as he stepped along in front, set his bundle of grass on fire. The badger heard the flint striking, and asked: "What is that noise, 'Crack, crack'?"

"Oh, that is nothing." replied the rabbit; "I only said 'Crack, crack' because this mountain is called Crackling Mountain."

The fire soon spread in the bundle of dry grass. The badger, hearing the crackle of the burning grass, asked, "What is that?"

"Now we have come to the Burning Mountain," answered the rabbit.

By this time all the hair had been burned off the badger's back. He now knew what had happened by the smell of the smoke. Screaming with pain the badger ran as fast as he could to his hole.

"What an unlucky fellow you are!" said the rabbit. "I can't imagine how this happened! I will bring you some medicine which will heal your back quickly!"

The rabbit went away glad to think that the punishment had already begun. He hoped that the badger would die of his burns, for he felt that nothing could be too bad for the animal, who was guilty of murdering a poor, helpless woman who had trusted him. He went home and made an ointment by

The Farmer and the Badger

mixing some sauce and red pepper together.

He carried this to the badger, but before putting it on he told him that it would cause him great pain, but that he must bear it, because it was a wonderful medicine for burns and scalds and such wounds. The badger begged him to apply it. But no language can describe the agony of the badger as soon as the red pepper had been pasted over his sore back. He rolled over and over and howled loudly. The rabbit felt that the farmer's wife was beginning to be avenged.

The badger was in bed for about a month; but at last, in spite of the red pepper application, his burns healed and he got well. When the rabbit saw this, he thought of another plan by which he could compass the creature's death. So he went one day to pay the badger a visit and to congratulate him on his recovery. During the conversation the rabbit mentioned that he was going fishing, and described how pleasant it was when the weather was fine and the sea smooth.

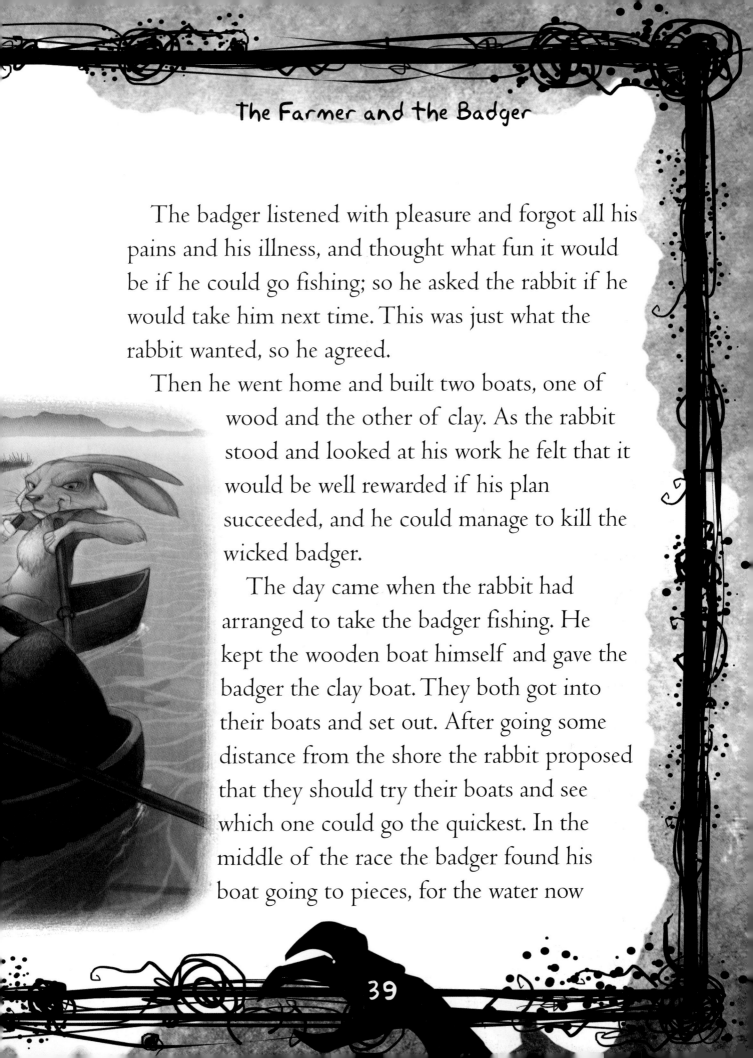

The badger listened with pleasure and forgot all his pains and his illness, and thought what fun it would be if he could go fishing; so he asked the rabbit if he would take him next time. This was just what the rabbit wanted, so he agreed.

Then he went home and built two boats, one of wood and the other of clay. As the rabbit stood and looked at his work he felt that it would be well rewarded if his plan succeeded, and he could manage to kill the wicked badger.

The day came when the rabbit had arranged to take the badger fishing. He kept the wooden boat himself and gave the badger the clay boat. They both got into their boats and set out. After going some distance from the shore the rabbit proposed that they should try their boats and see which one could go the quickest. In the middle of the race the badger found his boat going to pieces, for the water now began to soften the clay. He cried out in great fear to the rabbit to help him. But the rabbit answered that he was avenging the old woman's murder, and was happy to think that the badger had at last met his deserts for all his evil crimes. Then he raised his oar and struck at the badger till he fell with the sinking clay boat and was seen no more.

Thus at last he kept his promise to the old farmer. The rabbit now hurried back to tell him everything, and how the badger, his enemy, had been killed.

The old farmer thanked him with tears in his eyes. He said that till now he could never sleep at night or be at peace in the daytime, thinking of how his wife's death was unavenged, but from this time he would be able to sleep and eat as of old. He begged the rabbit to share his home, so from this day the rabbit went to stay with the old farmer and they both lived together as good friends to the end of their days.